INSPIRING TRUE STORIES BOOK FOR 9 YEAR OLD BOYS

I AM 9
AND
AMAZING

Inspirational tales About Courage, Self-Confidence and
Friendship

Paula Collins

Contents

Introduction

Hello, intrepid and wonderful boy! Did you know that you are exceptional? You are unique in the entire universe, which means there is no one like you in this vast world. That's truly amazing! Among billions of people, you have a special way of facing life. You are brave, funny, intelligent, and incredible. Never forget that.

In the world, you will find challenges of all sizes. Some may scare you, while others may make you doubt yourself. But remember, we all feel these emotions. Your parents, siblings, grandparents, friends, and even strangers feel the same as you.

Even when you face your fears, remember that you can overcome them and grow. When trying something new or facing difficult situations, you may feel fear at first, but the experiences that scare you the most often turn out to be the most valuable. Learn from your mistakes and find the goodness in everything you do, even when things are harder than you imagined.

In this book, you will find stories of children like you, brave and strong, who face situations similar to yours every day. They also feel fear and worry and sometimes don't win, but they work hard, keep trying, and learn from their mistakes until they achieve their goals.

When they feel discouraged or begin to doubt themselves, these children find that unique light within them that helps them keep going, even when they think about giving up. In each story, these children discover self-confidence, hope, and courage that allow them to live incredible experiences in every situation, leading them to reach their dreams.

Now is the time to light up your corner of the world. Share your light with others, free yourself from fear, and learn life's lessons. Believe in yourself, and you can accomplish anything.

You are an amazing and unique boy!

A Boy's Passion for Animals

Do you have a special place in your heart for animals? Did you know that many of them are looking for homes? Have you ever wondered about life in an animal shelter? This story is all about showing love and care for our furry friends.

Sam loved animals from a very young age. So when he saw a kitten nearby, he approached it and

touched it. Barely crawling, he moved, and as if touching the most delicate crystal in the world, he placed his little hand on it and caressed it. The cat responded with a meow, rubbing against his body. It was love at first sight.

So he grew up, and every animal he found in the street, he wanted to touch. Even his parents always took care that he did not approach a dangerous dog that could bite him or ask the owner's permission before he touched it.

Sam always had the touch to approach the animals; they saw his nobility and reacted with love. Even horses and dogs that were said to be aggressive with him would pull back their ears and begin to lick him.

When he was old enough to go to school and come up with ideas, he asked his mother to go to a shelter on Saturdays to help the animals. They began by doing simple tasks, such as taking several dogs for a walk, doing their business, collecting the waste in a bag, and returning them. They bathed some dogs and cats and even helped treat some of the injured animals that came in.

When he found sick or abandoned animals on the street, he would take them home and go to an adoption home. His mother asked him not to take

any more animals. There were already three dogs, four cats, and even a duck.

Everyone at school knew how much he loved animals. His best friend, Cory, was the opposite. He didn't like animals.

"I don't know how you can touch those animals full of bacteria and fleas," Cory said.

"I love animals; we all have bacteria, and your skin is as clean as it is. If I put it under a microscope right now, I will find several bacteria," Sam replied.

Cory would open his eyes like saucers and put on antibacterial. Sam shook his head. He loved his friend very much, but sometimes Cory was very delicate about hygiene and not touching animals because he thought they were monstrous things.

"We have to raise money," the woman from the shelter told him the next Saturday when they went to collaborate. "We are without resources, if we can't pay for the basics, we will go bankrupt, and I don't know what will happen to the animals' lives."

"How can I help?" Sam asked.

"Don't worry. You already do a lot for this shelter. You are the one who collaborates the most."

Sam didn't say anything, but he kept thinking all weekend about how he could help, what he could do to start generating money so that the shelter wouldn't close its doors. He thought about all those animals on the street who had been sacrificed.

On Sunday, when he went to bed, he had an idea in mind, and at dawn, as he was getting ready to go to school, he already had a clear idea.

At school, he told his friend Cory:

"I think I'll start selling things to help at the shelter."

"What are you going to sell? Your toys?"

"No. Mom made bracelets the other day with some little things they sold in bags. I think I'll buy them, put little letters on them, and make them personalized."

"Oh yes, but I don't know if anyone will buy them. You do a lot for all those animals."

"I don't do much. If I don't collaborate, it will close."

"Did they ask you?"

"No, I do it because I feel like it. Nobody helps those animals, as you say; for me, they are family."

After doing his homework, Sam began to prepare the bracelets. He made all kinds of bracelets, combining

colors, thinking about people's tastes, and after having a good material to sell, he came up against a big wall: how he would sell them. He had never offered things to other people; selling was a way to get out of his comfort zone, but he was afraid to offer.

"I know how much you love animals," his mother told him. "You've never sold anything. It's a bit embarrassing at first, but when you start offering them, little by little, you'll overcome that fear, and you'll see that it will become easier. You are afraid of it because it is something new for you."

Sam thought about it, faced his fear and the anxiety that was beginning to eat away at him, and told himself that the best way to confront fear was to put himself in front of it.

The school was the first place where he offered his products, first with his acquaintances; some classmates bought from him; and Cory supported him and bought from him, although not without adding a derogatory comment about animals.

Then he offered it to his teachers, and they all supported him because they knew it was for a good cause.

He then moved on to other teachers he did not know. Indeed, as he practiced, it became easier for him to sell. Soon he had clients asking him for personalized themes, which Sam gladly did.

Thus, a few days later, he had a large sum of money he had not imagined having so much of. The following week, when he went to the shelter, he brought it in a small box. It was a large sum in small bills. His fingers ached from all the bracelets he had made, but it was worth it. It was an effort for the animals.

When the woman from the shelter saw the money and learned how he had obtained it, her eyes watered.

"Sam, you didn't have to." she said, falling silent. She was about to cry; this whole sum was to pay the rent of the shelter and other things. Besides, we have received some donations. Thanks to you, we will be able to continue. I feel that this shelter is more yours than any of us. Thank you," she said, moving.

The following weeks, he continued to attend, although Sam thought of something interesting to convince Cory to go to the shelter on a Saturday.

"You don't have to touch animals, just see what I do. Come on, I'm sure you'll have fun."

"Fine," Cory said in the end; he knew that when his friend got something in his mind, no one could make him change his mind.

That weekend, Cory arrived early at Sam's house; he made his friend see that he had been quite punctual for not being interested.

"Alright, let's go see those animals and see how much you are attracted to them."

The mother started the car, and both boys sat in the back. On the way, Sam told him everything he was going to do. When they arrived, they got out with animal food, bags of soap for cleaning, and some medicine.

Sam felt at home. He lost himself in one of the rooms and started to do whatever was needed soon. Cory didn't want to touch anything; he felt that everything was dirty, or so he thought, although soon a yellow kitten approached him and started rubbing his legs and looking at him with love.

Something happened inside Cory, and he felt very deep love, and he knelt and started petting the cat.

Soon he adopted it, and although he had reservations about some chores like picking up dog waste, he became more of an animal lover and

named the cat Cooper, the first animal he loved with all his heart.

Sam did not miss helping the animals every Saturday, and Cory almost always accompanied him. When money was needed, Sam looked for a way to support them, and they organized different events.

All animals deserve love and need a lot of help because they live with us, and many are homeless.

Skating Dreams

Have you ever wanted to fulfill a dream with someone close to you, but only one achieves it? What did you feel when it happened? Joy or sadness? In this story, you will learn to see every day as a learning experience and that even if you don't always get what you want, it is already a triumph.

Michael and Max were two great friends; they had grown up together in the same community, and now they shared a dream to be skaters. Both of them

were dedicated to learning to reach great competition. Although Michael felt that he was not the best, he felt that Max moved around the rink with more ease.

"Come on, let's practice," Max told him.

"I'm scared. I don't want to."

"How can you be afraid if it's our dream?"

"It's just that I might not get it right."

"Come on, you'll see. We'll do it together."

Max did it without any problems, and Michael stumbled as he moved, but he defended himself in spite of everything.

They had to pass a test to see if they would compete in a race in their town, doing various pirouettes with the skates. Finally, the day of the test arrived.

When Max went out to the area where he would do the pirouettes, he moved from one side to the other. He felt he would fall at a certain moment, but he knew how to look good. He finished, and the jurors nodded. He felt he had done well.

Then it was Michael's turn, and when he stepped on the dance floor and received the order to start, he stood on the ice.

One of the jurors looked at him and winked, telling him to cheer up so he could start. Then, Michael saw Max, who saw him from afar and waved his hand to encourage him to continue.

"You can do it," said another juror.

"I'm sure you've practiced a lot," said another.

Michael became more and more encouraged and began to do it. Once, the skate slipped, and he fell, but he got on his knees, stood up, continued, and still did quite well.

The jury told them that both had been excellent.

Later, the jury chose only Max. Michael felt very sad, and without saying anything, he turned around and walked out. No one saw him, but tears were running down his cheeks.

Later, his father came looking for him, and seeing him so sad, he knew he had not made it.

"My son, I see you didn't do well. I'm sorry."

"Max was accepted."

"Oh, did you congratulate him?"

Michael thought about how he had left and did not even say goodbye to him. Now he had mixed feelings because he was happy for his friend, but at the same time, he was sad that he had not been accepted.

His father, guessing what he was feeling, said to him:

"It's okay to feel a little sad about what happened, but you also have to be happy for your friend and let him know so that he doesn't think you are full of envy and angry with him. Tell him that you are for him and that you are very happy for him."

That same night, Michael went to Max's house, and when he saw him, he jumped up and gave him a big hug.

"I'm sorry I left like that. I'm so glad they chose you."

"It's okay; I wanted to talk to you."

"What's wrong?"

"I don't think I want to do that. They accepted me, but I think I'm missing."

"What do you say? You're the best."

"I don't know if you noticed that I almost fell down."

"No, you looked great."

"Well, I struggled, I almost fell, and I feel like I'm lacking the skills to skate like those pros."

Max was glad to have his friend for support.

For the next few weeks, Michael would accompany his friend to skate, watching him move gracefully all over the place, jumping and sliding, correcting mistakes, and helping him improve.

But now something was happening. The more Max rehearsed and the closer the day came to competing with the other pros, the more mistakes he made. Apparently, due to nerves,

"I don't think I'm going to participate, he said to Michael."

"Of course, you will."

"Look how I'm making mistakes. I don't want to."

"It's nerves. You're terrific, trust you."

"I'll ask the jury to accept you in my place."

"You won't do that, he told him. You were chosen for a reason. I'll be by your side, supporting you."

"If it wasn't because you support me and are by my side, maybe I wouldn't have continued rehearsing one more day. You have helped me believe in getting to the final of the competition."

"That's what friends are for."

"Not all friends are like you."

"Not all of them are as good skaters as you are. You've had that passion for doing things, and that's why you were chosen, and you will surely win."

Every day, the two kept practicing and moving, even to make Max feel more confident. Michael put on his skates and started skating with him, moving through all the spaces and making the same moves as his friend.

Sometimes Michael did better than Max, and sometimes it was the other way around, but the two had an amazing time and were able to rehearse. Michael would keep that rehearsal for when he competed again to be chosen, and Max would be more confident and have a chance to win.

For the last days of rehearsals, they had a teacher from the same organization who would dedicate a few hours to him so that he could practice more fluently and correct mistakes. Those days, Michael

did not skate, but he watched his friend, listened to his advice, and then applied it on his own, learning more and being a support for Max.

There were days when the person who coached them stayed later to help him improve. With just one day left before the competition, the coach appeared with a smile and called Michael to come to his side. Very happily, he announced:

"I know you two are great friends, and I know how much you have helped your friend. You have really hit it off, and Max told me that without you, he would not have gotten to where he is today. So I was talking with the organization, and that is why I am bringing you great news today."

The two friends looked at each other with broad smiles as if guessing what it was about, although they didn't want to get ahead of themselves.

"The two of you will be able to compete, as I know you're doing quite well yourself. I hope you are happy about this news."

Michael began to jump for joy, for, of course, he wanted to participate.

The two friends began to dance with each other and give each other a big hug. They were extremely excited about being together.

On the day of the competition, they both participated and gave their best. Michael, who had been nervous at the beginning, felt confident and supported his friend, who also encouraged him to do it.

They both did excellently and went home happy and supportive of each other.

It went much better than they expected, and even the teacher who coached them at the end was surprised by the two of them and told them not to stop rehearsing to compete at the national level.

It is okay to feel sad in some situations when others get the same thing we compete for, but that should not be a reason to get angry or not want to see that person. Now we must show and support them.

When you support others in their dreams, you become stronger and thus achieve yours.

The Great Baking Challenge

Have you ever dreamed of entering a contest and coming out on top? Ever felt torn about which of your creations shines the brightest? Dive into this story to discover important lessons and find inspiration to believe in yourself even more.

A cooking contest was opened to see who made the best cakes and pastry recipes. It was open to all

children. The winner would get an oven for their home, identical to that of Tom, a little boy who wanted to participate and had always dreamed of it.

Although he was very happy, he was also nervous about participating because of everything that could happen. He wanted to make the perfect recipe, and the plan was to bake his shortbread cookies. He had always been good at it.

So, he started preparing the recipes.

Tom had a lot of excitement, but nerves got the better of him at many points. While he was cooking, his father appeared in the kitchen and saw him.

"What are you doing?"

"I'm making cakes."

"Why don't you make the cookies we like?"

"I want to use my best recipe so we can win that awesome oven! It's a super cool MagicBake oven they're giving away!"

That was the best oven on the market at the time, and the most expensive.

Tom stirred the mixtures. One for the batter, one to make the sprinkles, and one to fluff everything up.

"You should have made the chocolate pecan cakes that are so delicious. I remember they were amazing—the best I've ever tasted."

"I'm not going to make those cakes, Dad, because cakes are what everyone else is going to make, and I don't want to be one more with the same thing. I have to do something that will make me stand out from the others and increase my chances of winning."

"It's just that no one else can make these cakes like that; maybe others do, but no one like you, not even I, who have tried to copy the recipe, can make them as well as you."

He continued working on making the best cookies and made a series of batches of them. He saw that, in the end, he had different types, shapes, faces, animals, Christmas, and even Halloween themes.

As he went along, he realized that he had prepared a lot and couldn't decide on any of them. They all looked great, and the more he baked and took out cookie models, the more anxiety and sadness he felt. Something deep inside told him that he had not chosen the best option.

When the day of the contest arrived, he would bring the dough and cookies, as well as several other

ingredients that he would use to prove that he was the one preparing the recipe. Everyone lined up at a large table that had many stoves behind it, where each child would cook.

Each one of the judges was checking with the timer, ready for each child to start making their dessert.

In the middle of everything was the grand jury, who would taste all the recipes and would have to decide who was the best. Tom wanted to surprise them.

Each one began to prepare their recipes, trying to comply with the main rule: have fun doing it.

With his apron on, Tom concentrated on his work, baking more and more cookies, but when he tasted them after taking them out of the oven, he felt that they were not as delicious as he expected. They didn't taste bad, but they weren't the best treat he had hoped for, either. He was beginning to feel very frustrated with each batch, and at one point, he wanted to throw everything away and go cry in his father's arms.

He saw other children next to him, and this made him feel more worried. They were confident and were preparing their recipes, which smelled delicious and looked very pretty. He even saw some covered with purple glitter and others with rainbow-like designs.

He continued to work on his cookies, but as he watched, he became very discouraged.

He saw the clock and inwardly began to scream in despair.

"I'm running out of time, and I can't get the cookies the way I want them."

Then he began to look for other options and found the recipe for the cakes that his father had given him, and now it seemed they could save him.

He began to prepare the dough and felt confident. He remembered the first time he made this recipe, which came out almost by accident, and everyone praised him at home for how delicious it was.

As he progressed through the recipe, he felt more confident and had them almost ready to bake.

By the time he put them in the oven, he felt confident, and soon they began to grow and take the shape he wanted. They looked like little brown clouds with sprinkles on top.

Everyone around him was looking at him, wondering what he was doing, as it seemed to smell so good.

The stopwatch beeped, the time was up, and it was time to start testing and choosing the best recipe.

As the judges began to look at each preparation, they began to make comments:

"This with glitter looks great, but I think they burned a little, and this one was raw."

He went to another booth and tried another one.

"These cookies are delicious, although their appearance is not the best."

So, he went looking at them one by one until he got to Tom's table and saw the cakes, which he thought were delicious.

This smells great and looks spectacular.

He took one and took a bite. Tom could see how the flour sank when he bit into it. They were good.

The man made a strange grimace, and Tom swallowed saliva. He hadn't expected him to react like that.

"What a curious taste; I have never eaten anything like it."

Tom had expected the criticism since he had done this at the last minute.

"I think it's the best cake I've ever eaten in my life since my grandmother made them for me as a child. I've never eaten anything so delicious!"

Tom felt his heart leap out of his chest, and he jumped.

The man whispered something in his ear.

"Do you know why you won?"

"Because of my recipe."

"It's a great reason, but I chose you because many people forgot the key rule: have fun."

He felt he had to come clean.

"I confess that at the beginning I didn't have much fun."

"What changed?"

"I don't know. I think it was the recipe. I like making them, and even my dad recommended that I choose her for the recipe, but I didn't do it until the end."

"Well, it was certainly a great recommendation."

He saw everyone and said,

"We have the winner for making the most delicious cake I have ever eaten."

Everyone cheered and clapped happily.

As Tom had made quite a few cakes, they shared, and the others agreed that they were delicious. They shared them with milk and toasted the new winner.

That day, his father welcomed him with a big hug and helped him load the giant oven. The next problem would be figuring out where to put it at home, but this was one of those fun problems.

The message of this cute story is that while you are chasing your dreams, don't forget to have fun too.

Remember to smile and laugh when you are making efforts to achieve your goals. If you don't, you may end up with cookies you don't like and not-delicious cupcakes.

The Jelly Masterpieces of a Young Artist

Do you dream of doing something but think you won't make it because you're too young? Have you ever thought that maybe if you were faster, bigger, taller, or stronger, you could do such a thing? These are thoughts that hold you back, and that's what this story is about.

Liam was looking at the design in front of him. It didn't quite fit; he took an orange piece and arranged it differently, and it seemed to look better to his taste. When he removed the palette with which he moved each piece, he felt better with the result, and now he was smiling.

His mother was next to him and saw him smiling.

"I like the way it turned out."

"It's beautiful, son. I can't wait for us to devour it."

Liam was looking at what he had made: a design of different flavored jellies that formed a castle, with the tops of the towers orange and the rest blue, with bubble gum jelly, red jelly for flags, and so on.

That's what Liam was dedicated to, and he loved making art with gelatin.

He dreamed of being able to participate in an annual gelatin contest where they showed the best designs. They even had a Guinness record for the biggest gelatin in the world.

He wanted to win the best design.

He was just starting to clean his utensils when his younger brother, Charlie, walked in. Both had blonde, slightly wavy hair. His brother was bringing

him a flyer he had picked up on the street that talked about the baking contest where the artfully made gelatins could also go, and Liam would participate.

Liam watched his brother think about what he was saying, assimilating what he was proposing. Then he turned his attention to what the flyer was saying before answering something.

All the children in the city will be able to participate in a baking and jelly contest.

He glanced over to where they were talking about gelatin.

Those who make art with gelatin will be able to participate, and the winner will receive a monthly batch of ingredients for a year so they can let their creativity run wild.

Liam saw his brother and let out a shout of excitement.

"Can you imagine all the things I could cook and make with a year's supply? I could compete on a grand scale!"

"You're the best," Charlie told him.

"Thank you."

"You're going to win. Just look at that castle. It makes me want to bring the action figures and play."

The two boys screamed with excitement, and Mom asked them to calm down because they would alert all the neighbors.

The two brothers went to the living room to play and dream of all the things they could achieve if they continued with this contest. Liam saw the paper announcing the contest and could not believe it. He had just thought about it, and now he had the announcement in his hands.

He saw that he had to fill in some information to be able to participate and apply for the competition. Usually, he had to fill in the data, experience, age, and other things that his mother would surely help him to complete. The plan was for him to pick everything up and take it to an address that was indicated in the small print.

Charlie started dancing again, but Liam was left wondering if he could participate if it was his turn to put in all that data, but his mother reassured him and told him that she would help him fill it all out.

Mom, seeing him worried, asked him what he had:

"What if I'm too young?"

"That's silly; you're not. You make beautiful and delicious jellies, and you'll see how you win."

Charlie also encouraged him, and Liam felt he was luckier for having the two of them to help him push himself.

His mother gently lifted his chin and said with a warm smile, "You have what it takes to win this contest. Ever since I first let you help in the kitchen, you've shown such creativity. I truly believe in your talent." Liam nodded, his thoughts swirling despite her reassuring words.

The day of the competition came soon. Liam didn't know what he would have to do on the site, and besides, this contest was three rounds; he was already clear about what he would do in the first round, but not in the second, and even less for the third.

He was nervous; sometimes, when he would make jelly, it would look great, but he was afraid it would look bad or a piece would melt and ruin everything.

The mother told him it was normal to be afraid.

"All you do is practice, and in the competition, you will do your best, but whatever happens, there will always be another competition, and you will learn

from it, whether you win or not. You will learn; don't forget that."

Liam smiled at her; he understood the message.

The day of the contest was here, and he got ready. He put on his apron and took a deep breath, excited to start.

He saw many people and knew they'd be on TV. This made him a little nervous, but he calmed himself. A nice host came up, said hello to everyone, and asked if they were ready. All the kids shouted with joy. Now it was time to cook!

In one area, there were some boys and girls making cakes, and in Liam's area, they were all with jellies of various shapes ready to assemble.

Liam grabbed his tools and opened the cellar, in which he had a whole arsenal of jellies of all sizes and shapes, so that, like a lego, he began to assemble each piece and form figures.

He measured, assembled, and leveled each piece. Until what he wanted was taking shape. He waited to adhere and glue what he wanted, praying that nothing would be ruined.

As he prepared his jellies, he calmed down, and his nerves no longer controlled him. Then he realized that he did belong in this contest, even if he was the youngest of them all.

He did well in the first round and better in the second. Liam made a giant robot that surprised everyone with how it could stand up. He didn't tell everyone that the secret was in the consistency of the gelatin, so that it wouldn't move so much.

He was very proud of the decorations; he made small balls by chopping them and putting them as a kind of lamp in a colonial-era house with thick walls; he combined neutral colors with bright colors; and the final trick was small pieces of gelatin that looked like tiles. With this, he achieved an old house that looked very realistic.

The contest ended, and the winners were announced. The first one went to a boy who made a famous TV doll that looked very realistic. When the judges saw Liam's art, they winked at him and moved on.

Now it was time to see who the other winners would be. Liam's nerves were on edge. He closed his eyes, praying that he would be one of them.

He heard another name that wasn't his, and then when there was only one left, he was even more nervous because the next one was the first place out of three.

"Liam!" said the cheerleader cheerfully.

He opened his eyes and smiled. He couldn't believe he was the winner of the competition. He smiled at his mother and brother, who were watching him from afar and were very happy, with tears running down their cheeks.

This would help Liam continue preparing himself to participate in more challenging competitions. Each competition would be a step toward growing and becoming better at his art.

Believe in yourself and the gifts you have. Remember, when you chase your dreams, amazing things can happen. Follow your heart, and don't just wait for good things to come your way. Dream big and work hard for what you want.

United by Soccer

You probably know many things in life that you are passionate about, but do you know everything about them? Can you find out more about what you love? Surely you can, and that's what the story below is all about, where one character discovers how you can learn more every day.

James was very good at what he did. Soccer ran through his veins, and when he got on the field, he

moved very quickly with the ball, held the team's goal-scoring record, and was proud of it.

One day, at his practice, he was playing a game. He started running all over the field with the ball, dodged every single opponent, turned a deaf ear to his teammates' request to pass him the ball, reached the other team's goal, and scored an extraordinary goal.

Everyone applauded the goal and continued the game. Several goals were repeated, with him controlling the ball and not thinking about passing it to the others.

When the game was over, gathered in the dressing room, the coach said, "It was a very good game today, but James was the one who made the most mistakes."

"But I scored all the goals," James protested.

"You are not the only one on the field. The whole game, they were asking you to pass the ball, and you ignored everyone. Even me."

"But the others don't score goals like me."

"It's a team game, 'soccer team,' not 'soccer James.'"

James was very upset and said no more. The coach spent the rest of the conversation talking to the

others about the game and what they could improve on.

James's father, who was there, came over and said to him alone, "Son, I have raised you kindly, and you are kind, but when you are playing, you are selfish, and you don't know how to work as a team. It hurts me to say it, but the coach is right. You have to think about that."

The next day, the coach got them all together to talk about what he would do. Everything seemed as usual, although what felt strange was that next to the coach, there was a boy he had never seen before. He belonged to the team because he had the ball in his hands, and he looked at them all with a calm air.

"Guys, this is Sam; he has just joined the locality and the team, well, he wants to join. He has shown in a meeting we had that he has talent and can be a good added value for us. I want you to welcome him, and he will start practicing today."

They all cheered, except James.

James didn't know what to think when he saw this new boy on the team.

When they were on the field, the coach gave James a different position than usual. He normally played forward, but now he put him somewhere else.

"Coach, I want to be a forward."

"I know, but we are testing Sam to see where he performs best. We have to do it for the team."

James thought about what his father had said and swallowed. He turned and went to his position. When the coach blew the whistle, the boys began to move, and Sam was moving incredibly well, soon teaming up with the others. He scored a goal.

James realized that Sam was better at playing than he was.

When the practice was over, James was impressed by everything Sam had done—some moves he didn't know how to do, even some shots he thought were impossible—and Sam did them as if he were used to them. It would be hard to keep up with the newcomer.

On the way home from practice, James asked his father:

"I have a question, dad. What do you do when someone is better than you at something?"

His father looked at him and then said,

"Well," he said taking a moment, "someone will always be better than you at what you do, even at what you love most in the world. It's just the way it works, but you can strive to become better and learn more."

James nodded and kept thinking, guessing he would have to do that.

James spent that night and day at school thinking about it, not sure how he was going to learn more about soccer. He thought he knew everything.

In the end, he deduced that he would probably have to have a conversation with the coach. As much as James didn't like to admit it, he didn't know what the other step would be. The coach could clear it all up for him.

He arrived early for training. He inhaled and faced the fear of talking to the coach.

"Hello, coach," he said to him. "I hope you are very well. Can I ask you something?"

The coach smiled and said,

"Thank you for asking how I am and for seeking to be polite. It is good that now you see the signs that I have been trying to teach you for a long time."

James looked at him and bitterly said:

"That Sam is better than me."

"No, that's not what I would say. What I would say is that both of you have different skills."

"All right, how do I get it? I want to be like him."

"I think the person who could help you best with this is Sam himself. Talk to him."

"Talk to him?"

"I think you can learn something from each other, you can even be good friends."

James looked at him for a few seconds and then said,

"I think you're right. I'll talk to him as soon as I see him."

The trainer let out a laugh and said,

"If I had known that just by bringing a player to the team, you would notice so many things, I would have added him months ago."

The coach smiled with tenderness and a bit of amusement and walked away as he said, "I'm glad you're excited about all this. I knew you would be."

James found Sam on the field. He was with a ball, moving it around and making some moves.

"Hi," he said to him.

"Hi."

"I'm James."

"Okay, I'm Sam. Are we on the same team?"

They both introduced themselves, and he soon learned that they went to the same school and that Sam had some doubts about statistics and could use some help. When they had talked a bit, James said to him:

"Do you think we could play soccer so you could show me some of those moves you did yesterday? They're great, and I don't know them."

"Sure, I think that's a great idea."

"That's great, we'll learn things."

"Sure, you probably know things that I don't. How about after practice?"

James nodded, happy.

"It would be great if we could play together later."

From that day on, Sam and James became friends. They were united by soccer and always met after class to play for a while and learn more.

They would be friends for the rest of their lives.

Never stop learning, whether you know it or not. Every day, you remember and learn a little bit of everything, even the things you think you know the most. You will never stop learning. When you think you have all the information, new knowledge will appear, and someone who knows more than you will appear.

The Distracted Boy

Do you easily get lost in something that interests you and don't see what's going on around you? Does your time slip by without you noticing, and then you hurry?

This is the story of Jack, a boy who loved to walk and see how the world worked but learned a lesson a little rudely.

The city where Jack lived was the quietest in the world, so quiet that stores and businesses didn't lock up at night, there were no thieves, and there were no bad people. That's why he could go to and from school without his parents. He did it when he was seven years old. So, the little boy went with his backpack on his shoulder, the snacks on one side, and walked, hopping and enjoying the things along the way.

Although there was a problem that arose soon after he started going on his own, although he left in time to get to school in time to play with his friends, he would arrive late, even half an hour after classes had started.

The first few days, he was told nothing, but when it became a habit, the teacher called his mother.

"But if he comes early enough, I don't send him late." The mother said this when they complained to her.

"Because every day he is very late, and this can affect his school performance." said the teacher.

When the mother spoke to Jack, he said with a broad smile:

"I'm going straight to school, the way you taught me."

"Why are you late? I know your legs are smaller than mine, but it's close to home; you could be there in ten minutes, and you leave 40 minutes earlier. What's wrong?"

"I don't know; I'm leaving; I see things; I walk; I greet people, mom."

"The other day, I saw how they were carrying a giant clock up a window, three men, and a rope. They almost dropped it; it took them a long time to carry it up."

The mother was beginning to understand what was happening. Her son was getting careless and wandering around the world, seeing everything around him, and time was passing by without him noticing.

"Son, I know you like to see everything around you, but you can't stay like that, lost, because then you'll be late, and you'll see the consequences."

"But that watch was so funny, I liked it. It's not my fault that they make things so interesting."

"But you're late every day, according to the teacher."

"Days ago, I saw a duck with a lot of ducklings, and the children almost fell into a sewer. I followed them

to help them if something happened to them—a poor mother with so many children."

"You are a boy with a good heart, but remember that there are consequences if you leave like that. Don't do it, son. Do you promise me that you will concentrate on getting to school faster and on time?"

"I promise, Mom."

The next day, while Jack was getting ready, he thought about how he would not stop to see everything interesting on the street. What a waste of time. His mother told him that he could do it on the way back, that there was more time, but not on the way there because he had to be on time. She told him that on the way back, there was almost nothing, just people eating lunch, as it was break time.

There was no way to get his mother to change her mind. He had to get to school early.

That day, he was on his way to school and came across a truck with something that looked like a diamond turning in the back. He knew it was concrete; he was attracted to it, and he saw some men working and pouring some columns. It was interesting, but he sighed and kept walking. He couldn't dawdle.

Up ahead, as he walked on, he saw the most beautiful dog he had ever encountered, with white fur that looked like cotton and eyes as blue as the sky. It had a home because on its head was a blue bow. When it saw him, it stood up and wagged its tail so he could pet it. Jack stopped and petted it gently, and he let go. He was tempted to stay there for a while but thought about the promise and kept moving forward after saying goodbye to the canine.

"I'm sorry, buddy, I have to go to class."

The following days, he was very judicious, following the rules that his mother asked him and arriving on time to school. He knew he had to be punctual and responsible, but it weighed on him to miss many things on the way and to enjoy everything that the road had to offer, but it was part of the sacrifices to be responsible.

Some time passed, and he forgot his normal or slightly delayed regimen of compliance. He began to stay a little longer, calculating that he would get to class on time. As long as he got in on time, there was no problem with staying a while to watch something.

So, one day, he greeted the bricklayers and watched them work. On another occasion, he greeted a dog. He met the duck and ducklings who were older and

took the bread out of his backpack and shared it with them.

He watched the clock, and when he was on time, he left at a fast pace and arrived at school on time. With that, there were no problems, and he complied with everyone.

One day, he met the white dog again and devoted himself to spoiling it. It seemed like love at first sight. He began to pet it and talk to it, and the little animal wagged its tail at him.

Time slipped away, and before he knew it, only 3 minutes remained for him to get to school. At his regular pace, he'd need at least 7 minutes to make it. He'd have to sprint if he wanted to avoid being tardy. After saying goodbye to the dog, he bolted out the door. As he approached the corner, he was in such a rush that he didn't notice the uneven sidewalk ahead. Suddenly, he tripped and fell hard, scraping his knees.

Slowly, he looked up to find a concerned passerby offering him a hand. "Are you okay, buddy?" the man asked.

His vision blurred from the tears that welled up, not from the pain of the fall but from the embarrassment and shock. Just then, he heard his mother's voice,

filled with concern: "Oh, sweetheart, you have to be careful!"

Helping him up, she inspected his scraped knees, which were starting to bleed a little. "We should get you home and clean these up," she said gently.

Reflecting on the incident, he realized he had been so focused on not being late that he forgot to pay attention to his surroundings. His mother's words resonated with him: "It's better to lose a minute in life than to risk your well-being."

She reminded him that his promise to be punctual for school had led him to this rush and fall. From then on, he vowed not to be distracted along the way so as not to be late.

Always remember: hurrying can lead to unintended consequences, and it's essential to be aware of your surroundings at all times.

The Bonsai Adventure

Have you ever felt like you spend time with the people you love and wish you could enjoy them more? Do you have unforgettable memories with family members? When you learn more about them, you can enjoy many things. This is a story where a grandson and his grandfather have a great adventure.

Everything he saw around him was beautiful: little stalls with lots of things to entertain, bonsai trees of all kinds, smoke in the background of the food court, a colorful world of plants that went from tiny seeds to works of art that came from generation to generation.

Michael was watching in wonder at that work. He knew that to get to where he was, they had worked very hard. Well, with the grandfather who was by his side, they went through many adventures, but it had been worth it.

"Do you like it?" asked his grandfather.

Michael nodded his head; no doubt he liked it.

A few days ago, he was with his grandfather at his house. He had stayed a few days because he had school vacations. His parents had left him there so they could share, and for Michael, these were the happiest moments of his life.

Grandpa had a beautiful garden at the back of the house. He was surprised at how good he was at taking care of plants; not a single leaf was dry, and all of them were bright green, attractive, and full of life. The bonsai trees seemed to vibrate when he approached them, and grandpa had the habit of hugging them and kissing them when he poured water on them. He told them that they were very

beautiful that day and that the tree he had poured was the most beautiful of all.

"Why do you talk to the trees, Grandpa?"

"They feel."

"But they don't listen."

"No, they don't listen to us, I think, but they do feel our good energy. If you come and show them that love, they will show it by becoming beautiful like that."

Michael went into his grandfather's room, and there he saw a collection of bonsai trees in various stages of growth. He was amazed at how much work was involved.

He touched one of the bonsai trees and found it very beautiful and delicate, with the branches carefully shaped and the leaves trimmed to perfection.

"What is all this, Grandpa?"

"It's an art form that I'm sure you'll love. It's bonsai, the art of growing and shaping miniature trees."

"They're beautiful."

"Thank you, my boy."

He saw all the different types of bonsai trees.

"Did you do them all?"

"Yes, they are my work and my effort."

"I can tell. I can't imagine how you can do that; it's so intricate with so many details."

"It's done with patience and care, following specific techniques and methods. And so the shape emerges."

"What is that for?"

"For everything, I can even create a bonsai tree to represent a special memory or occasion. I can also shape them into different forms, like animals or symbols. You name it."

"But you have a lot."

Grandpa laughed.

"Yes, I have to create these for a fair that is coming soon, and I will show everyone my work to sell them. Many are going to buy them to put them in their homes."

"Can I go with you to that fair?"

"Of course, you can. I hope you will come with me."

"I want to learn about bonsai."

"I promise that soon we'll both start doing it, and I'll teach you."

Michael looked at all the bonsai trees. Some he liked, others he didn't.

"I want you to help me choose which ones to take to the fair."

"I like the one shaped like a dragon."

"Okay, we'll take it."

"I love that one with the twisted trunk."

"That one goes."

And so they selected each one of the bonsai trees. They were selecting different types of designs to display and take to the fair. Simple designs, some more elaborate, and everything to make it look like an incredible exhibit.

"Let's take all this to the car, but first, let's pack the bonsai trees carefully so we can keep them safe and secure."

Michael took the box that his grandfather showed him and began to pack what he told him. He did it

with a lot of order because he wanted everything to arrive perfectly.

Everything was packed with much love, and they both left to take it to the car. The grandfather opened the trunk, and Michael carried in his arms a box with the most important bonsai trees. He felt valuable doing that.

But suddenly, carrying the box, he tripped and fell, sitting down. To his bad luck, the box flew through the air and fell right onto the ground, spilling the bonsai trees and breaking some of the pots.

"It can't be! I'm so sorry, Grandpa, I'm sorry."

Michael's eyes burned, and he immediately began to cry. He felt guilty, for the best bonsai trees were now damaged, and they could not be sold. He began to pick them up, and they looked broken, for the pots were shattered and the branches bent.

Grandpa calmed Michael down and told him not to worry. They would fix it.

They went back into the house and began to select other bonsai trees, although they didn't like them as much.

"We'll have to create something new. Come. I'll show you."

Grandpa took a small tree and a pot and told him.

"You will start shaping this tree, following my guidance."

He showed Michael how to trim the branches and shape the tree, and soon, Michael had created a unique and beautiful bonsai tree.

"What is the design?"

"Let your heart speak to you."

Michael shaped the tree, following his instincts and letting himself go. He wanted to make a unique bonsai tree that would be the main attraction at the fair.

The design was taking shape, and although he worked and worked, after a while, he felt that it was not what he expected. For a moment, it seemed like an animal was emerging, then it was something abstract, and then it looked like a small forest. It was strange.

Grandpa was working quickly on fixing the damaged bonsai trees; for now, they needed more trees for the fair.

What had been broken was being repaired, but surely the buyers would notice that they had been damaged and would think they were not as valuable.

He continued shaping his tree, and at the end, he saw a strange shape that he didn't understand. It was a unique and eye-catching design.

He was going to cry; he thought that now he had wasted a tree, but Grandpa looked at him.

"What have you got?"

"I ruined it again."

"You didn't ruin anything; it was an accident. He looked at him sweetly. Show me that design."

Grandpa took it and said:

"You have a talent for this; you've created something unique and beautiful."

The next day was the fair, and they exhibited the bonsai trees along with the others. Michael was surprised that his unique tree was a sensation for everyone. Whoever stopped to look at the stand had to say something positive about the tree.

Finally, someone bought it, and then others came looking for more.

"Without that mistake, you would never have discovered that talent, nor would they have stopped to see the things here. You see, your unique tree stole the show of the whole fair."

Michael felt happy and fortunate.

For Michael, it was a great experience; although accidents can happen, if you dare to make things, you reinvent yourself and end up with something as beautiful as Michael's unique bonsai tree.

When you make mistakes, beautiful things can turn out in the end. Grandparents are the best thing that can happen to us in life. If you are lucky, you can help them with their things, and you get fantastic experiences. It doesn't matter how old you are. Enjoy them.

The Lesson for the Know-It-All Boy

Has it ever happened to you that you know everything and share it with the world? Or have you met someone who shows that they know it all and want to steal the show by going over everyone else's head? Discover this story where a little boy learns a great lesson.

Sam always stood out wherever he was, not only because he was a charming little boy and always talking, but because he interrupted and shared his wisdom even with those who didn't want to know it.

In the classroom, when the teacher asked a question, everyone waited for his answer because he was the one who knew when the Spaniards had touched American soil, the beginning of the French Revolution, or how many days the 100-day war lasted. He knew them all, and for those he didn't know, he looked for an answer and solved them.

Although this was good because he could solve the big doubts, sometimes it was not so good. When the teacher asked a child something, he would interrupt and answer for him, even if this answer was worth points and he had already answered his turn.

"You know you can't be answering for others," the teacher would tell him sternly.

Sam would nod his head, keep silent, but then interrupt again and give his opinion. The teacher would threaten to punish him or subtract a point, but for him, it was no problem because the pleasure of being able to answer was what most encouraged him to interrupt.

Although it was not only in class that he interrupted in this way, he also did it at recess with his friends. For example, on one occasion, a friend was telling a story that had happened to him at home, and since Sam already knew it, he interrupted him and told it to him when he had nothing to say.

"Sam!" said the boy who was telling the story.

"What?"

"You told my story."

"Ah, it's just that I tell it better."

"You can't tell it better, and even if you could, it's my story anyway; you don't have to interfere."

"But it was just the story. Go on, finish telling it yourself."

That's how it was with all his friends, they knew that he interrupted and that he always wanted to say things about others, although they also knew that he was a good, noble, and cooperative boy, and that's why they accepted him despite his great flaw.

At home, he also went through the same situation. He answered for his father, his mother, his siblings, his uncle, his cousin, his grandmother, and even for the dog because once he watered something, his

mother asked the animal why she did it, and he said that it was when she was jumping happily with her paw that she had knocked it down.

He would get into everything.

"One day, this is going to cause you a problem, and you are going to have a lesson where you will learn that you don't know everything." said his mom.

"If that day comes, I'll learn something. You just said so, Mom."

The mother raised her eyes, and her son was very passionate about it.

Besides, he had a habit of reading, and he knew a lot of things that easily stuck with him.

The next day, he would share it at school with his friends; they would listen to his anecdotes about World War II and other very interesting topics.

One day, when he arrived at class, there was a large computer with a big screen. When Sam saw it, he felt that his eyes were shining and that it was his opportunity to demonstrate what he had learned in a computer course he had taken some time ago.

The teacher was trying to play an educational video with animated characters. Rumor had circulated in

town that this was educational but a lot of fun, and all the kids were talking about them, although there was no information on the internet, and they were looking forward to watching it.

The teacher was passing out papers so she could get in and play the video.

"I know!" said Sam, who got up and went to look at the computer.

"Oh no!" said a couple of children.

"He's going to break it," said another.

"Goodbye video, whispered someone."

"As far as I know, don't start," said Sam.

He opened the file and double-clicked it to open, but something happened to the computer that closed it; the other windows closed and the screen went black; the image that was projected on the wall went off too; and everyone emitted an

"Noooo!"

"You always want to know them all, and these things happen. You're grounded," said the teacher, who looked annoyed.

Sam, surprised to see everyone's reaction, obeyed and went to his seat in the classroom.

Someone from Systems came soon and repaired the computer, and they watched the video. From a distance, Sam silently watched it, although he had a bad taste for everything that had happened.

Later, he would find out that he was also grounded. He would have to figure something out.

"If you want to go home, you will have to solve this puzzle since you know them all." said the teacher when she handed him a box, which, according to her, opened in several parts.

Sam, feeling a little arrogant, began to move the cube all over the place, looking for a crack. He squeezed it, shook it, and hit it against the wall, but he had no luck; it wouldn't come apart, and time went by while he became more and more frustrated, first because the puzzle didn't advance, which made him stay longer, and second because he didn't know that, he had always been good at solving puzzles and looking for answers, now, something so elementary, he couldn't solve it.

The teacher came in a long time later. Sam was sitting, looking at the cube with frustration. The

teacher picked it up with her fingertips, moved them one on each side, and the cube clicked and fell apart.

"How did you do it?"

"I learned, I played, I practiced, and I did it. It had its shape, so I could do it, but that wasn't the lesson."

"So?"

"Well, you don't always know them all. You have to learn that you can't always answer everything and that even when you try to put your hand where you shouldn't, you can mess things up."

"It's not like that."

"I've often had to rephrase questions because you answer the ones I've prepared in advance to evaluate your peers. It's good that you learn things, but you can't interrupt others to show that you know. We all know you're smart."

Sam reflected on what his teacher told him. After this, she let him go home, but he thought about many things from his past—how he had reacted and what he had said. He realized that his attitude was not the best and that he had upset many.

From that day on, he always waited for his classmates to ask him for the answer; for example,

when the teacher asked in which era Caligula had lived, he remained silent; when no one answered, they looked at him, and he answered. At home, it was the same. He never meddled again. He learned that being silent was also wise and that a wagon that goes down the street sounds empty because it is empty. When it is full, it doesn't make so much noise.

Now Sam knows that to be silent, to reflect, and to participate with his wisdom in good times is part of respecting others.

It is good to know a lot, but sharing it or interrupting others to show what you know will only leave you with bad experiences. Nobody likes to be answered or interrupted.

Wise people are the ones who talk the least; wanting to get attention by taking it away from others will only leave you with bad experiences.

The lesson for the know-it-All boy teaches us the importance of humility and respect for others. While it's great to be knowledgeable, it's also essential to listen and allow others to express themselves.

The Younger Brother and the Bike Contest

Have you ever had to make difficult decisions and didn't know what to do? Sometimes we have to choose difficult things, and we must know how to do it correctly and choose the most important one. This story will teach you that.

Ethan loved his brother very much, and wherever he went, he always went with him. He was the older

brother, so he took care of him and made sure he had everything he needed. When he came home from school, he would bring him a treat, and they would play together, download apps on the phone, and play games.

They spent many hours together as their parents worked, so even though they were siblings, he sometimes acted as a big brother and a guardian.

One thing Liam, his younger brother, had taken a liking to was bicycles. He had been given one for his birthday and had learned quickly. Soon the training wheels were off, and he was riding from one side to the other like an expert. This made Ethan very proud, and he always told everyone.

Ethan wanted to give his best to his brother. He was his best friend, and so at the first call, he always came, and they played a lot. He was attentive to helping his parents educate him, like when he didn't want to eat, he sat next to him and made him eat everything, or if not, he made him forget about sweets.

One day they announced that a cycling competition was coming to town, and there was a section for children. Whoever participated and showed what they could do, there would be a gift just for

participating. All to promote the sport among the children.

Ethan was excited. He asked his parents for permission, and they said yes, to take him, as it would be a lot of fun for a child.

"Do you want to go to the bike contest?"

"Where is it?"

"nearby, in the park."

"Can I take the bike?"

"Of course! You're going to participate."

The boy started jumping up and down excitedly. He couldn't believe he would win a bike contest. He had only seen it in videos on the internet.

"Before we go, we'll spend the next few days rehearsing so you can do well, even though you already do it the best. So, when we get there, you'll be the best, and everyone will see you." Ethan told him.

They spent the next few days practicing in the backyard. Liam would get on the bike and start jumping from one side to the other; he would go up a bank, move forward, and when he braked, he

would turn the whole bike around. In this way, he was preparing himself to be the best; they even watched videos on the internet to find new things to do.

It was amazing how Liam learned so easily on the bike.

In this way, they both seemed to get smarter every day. Even though Liam was the one who was going to participate, as a teacher, Ethan helped him and gave him the best advice. They were both looking forward to participating.

Ethan had also checked the bike, and on the internet, he found out what needed to be done in maintenance. He put air in the tires, prepared the brakes, and tightened screws and nuts so that nothing was out of place.

Then they would begin a routine they had both prepared. Ethan told him how to warm up and prepare to move around the space with a circuit of various obstacles, and the plan was to overcome them in the shortest time possible and work hard on the ones where he still lacked experience.

Finally, they did an obstacle course on a single wheel. Ethan smiled so much that, in the end, Liam didn't even fall. Everything was perfect. He had learned very fast and felt like he was watching one of those live

shows on the sports channel where the cyclists did pirouettes.

Everything looks great so far. They even rehearsed in the rain because they could not make excuses for anything.

The day before the show, they had already prepared the bag and everything they needed. Liam ate dinner and started sneezing.

Half an hour later, he had a fever.

"I don't think Liam is well, Mom" told Ethan.

"Yes, I just saw him. I gave him some anti-allergic and his medicine to make him feel better. Did you get wet?"

"It rained these days, but we changed our clothes."

"He caught a cold. You know they can't get wet. Let's hope he feels better tomorrow."

"I hope so, because we're going to the contest.

"If he wakes up with a fever, it's time to take him to the doctor."

"Mom! But the contest"

"Well, part of being a big brother is that sometimes we have to make decisions that, even though we don't like, we know it's the best thing to do."

"What do we do?"

Ethan thought about everything. On the one hand, they had spent a lot of time on this contest. They wanted to show everyone how well Liam was doing on the bike, but if he woke up sick, they couldn't go to the competition because he could get worse because of the physical activity. Besides, Liam didn't look good. The truth was that he didn't even seem to be interested in this contest.

Ethan did his mental math and knew what was best.

"Yes, Liam should go to the doctor to see him if he wakes up sick."

The next day, the boy did indeed still have a fever. They went to the doctor first thing in the morning so that he could prescribe medicine that would cure him soon.

At home, Ethan was in the room with his little brother, and they ate together. Then he sat on an armchair there, and they talked until he fell asleep. He didn't notice that he also fell asleep and spent the night in the room close to his brother.

The next day, he woke up when he heard Liam shouting happily that he was feeling well and no more snot was coming out of his mouth. He was thirsty and hungry.

Ethan remembered that this was the day of the contest and that the time to arrive had already passed.

He turned on the television and began to see the children doing the pirouettes and demonstrating their talent. Shortly after, they were each given a prize: a beautiful toy, one of those that appeared on television.

Ethan spent some time thinking, and at the end, he said, "you know, we don't need to show off."

"You know, we don't need to prove that you're the best on the bike. We both know you are."

Liam smiled and nodded happily.

Soon after, the mother looked at the boy to confirm how he was feeling and was relieved to see that he had healed.

"You look good. Those medicines healed you quickly."

The mother saw Ethan and stood next to him, watching the TV screen. The children were still there, happy with their gifts.

"I know how hard you worked for this contest. But I am proud that you put your little brother's health first, and it is the best decision you made. Someday you will be a wonderful father, just like you are an amazing brother today."

Her mother kissed him on the cheek.

"Thank you, Mom. I'm so glad I had your help, and besides, next year we'll get ready, and we won't get ewt, so we can go to the contest and win."

Liam also agreed. The three of them spent that day having fun in the afternoon. They went out riding their bikes. They happily enjoyed themselves with other neighbors who had also gone to the contest.

They both took these training days as an experience where they had a lot of fun and also prepared themselves to be the best next year.

Ethan knew that he had to take care of his loved ones and the people he loved, and although sometimes we have to sacrifice something we have worked for, the reason is for greater causes, even if it hurts. It is the right thing to do.

The Power of Kind Words

Jack had a couple of friends on the same block who had been together since they were very little. Their parents would get together, and since they were babies, they would play. As they grew up, they learned to communicate with words, and today, at 7 and a half years old, they are the best friends in the world. They are always included in any plan. If the fair comes to town, the three of them have to go, or, failing that, the three families go; if there is something where they live, the three of them participate. They even study in the same classroom, so they do their homework together, and when they play in a group, who is the group? Exactly, them.

Oliver and Vince were the other two friends, and although they always got along well, there were times when Oliver showed a strong personality and argued with them.

One day, when the three of them were playing at home, they made plans to play with action figures. When they combined that, Vince took out a toy car set, and in a few minutes, they set up a race track for their action figures. Oliver, who was the one with the idea, got first in line with his robot, a blue action figure he had had for a long time.

Jack had the action figure of a superhero and started arguing for his turn.

"My robot is ready to race," said Oliver.

"My superhero is too. Get in the back; don't be a cheater."

"I'm already here. Next time."

They both started to argue and push each other, and at the end, Oliver said:

"You're a bad boy. I don't want you anymore!"

He left the room, slammed the door, and went home.

"Are you all right?" Vince asked him.

"Sometimes it bothers me when Oliver says mean things to us," said Jack.

"Yes, he's hurtful with words; he's said a lot of things to me."

"I'm sure when he calms down, he'll come to apologize, but anyway, what he said leaves a mark."

"I understand you. I hope he will soon change his ways."

That same night, Oliver appeared in the room; his chin was low, and his eyes were big and sad. He looked at the two of them with an air of guilt.

"You were right," he said to Jack; "it was your turn. I should have stood in line. I did things wrong twice. I said ugly things to you."

"Don't worry, I forgive you," said Jack, "but try to work on not hurting others with your words."

They forgave each other and continued playing. Oliver behaved well and did not abuse his friends, and apparently, what had been said was forgotten.

The next day, Jack's mother gave her son some news:

"Oliver's mother called me."

"Okay, where are we going?" Jack said because that was always the beginning of his mother's plans, "Vince's mom called me, and we're going to the movies," or "Oliver's mom called me, and we're going to the beach for the weekend."

"Sorry, it's not a trip. Oliver is sick; he spent the night with a stomach ache and was vomiting this morning. The doctor saw him, and apparently, it was from something he had eaten. He reacted and is sick."

"Can we visit him?"

"Sure, I'll ask his mom."

Jack thought about what he could do to help his friend, what to bring to encourage him to feel better, and how to motivate him. Finally, he spent the day chewing over an idea that might work and also taught Oliver a lesson about how words have an influence.

He decided to create a letter for him, decorated it with everything cool he had in his room, put stickers on it, made drawings with markers, made a robot similar to his action figure, and inside, he wrote a message:

"You are the best friend in the world and the coolest; get well soon to play a lot."

That night, when they went to visit him, he gave it to him. They had never been that kind of detail, so it seemed strange to Oliver when he read the message; his eyes watered, and he said it was the nicest thing he had given him.

"Nice words fill the heart; get well soon," Jack told him.

"Yes, and hurtful words leave scars. I understood the message. Thank you, my friend. You make me feel better."

They continued sharing that night, and almost when Jack was about to leave, Oliver had a great idea:

"What if we created a card company with positive messages?"

"What are you talking about?"

Oliver explained that why not dedicate themselves to bringing lovely messages to people in need?

Jack loved the idea, and soon Vince was on board.

So, with no plans to make money, they began writing letters with positive messages to their neighbors, one

to their parents, to thank them for the effort they make every day.

Vince's grandmother got sick, and they wrote her something positive to help her feel better.

A neighbor had surgery, and a letter was sent to the hospital with one of the family members telling her that they hoped she would come home soon and get better.

A neighbor lost his pet because it was already a very old dog, and they gave him a card with an identical dog with white wings on its back. The man hugged them and thanked them, saying that it had been the most beautiful gift they had given him in his life.

Thus, in a few weeks, they had delivered many cards with messages full of love for people, for the sad ones, the ones who had lost someone important, the sick, and even congratulations, like the one given to Oliver's father when he found a job in a company he had always wanted as a career goal.

"Congratulations on your new job, you deserve it; I'm sure you'll give it your all," and they put his father working at a computer.

One day, Oliver got sick with a very strong viral flu. He infected Jack and also Vince; the three friends saw

each other by video call, and they had to stay in bed and take all their medicines. They were sad, with little spirit to do anything.

What a surprise it would be when the mother of each one brought a large letter, the size of a notebook. The cover of each one had a favorite character and many drawings, robots, superheroes, and a sports star. Inside, there were many messages with different letters.

There were many messages from the neighbors and friends they had helped with their letters. Now they wrote them messages asking them to get better soon, to take care of themselves, and that they missed them. The three of them cried with happiness when they had those messages full of love in their hands; they realized that words could heal and make them feel better.

Oliver understood that he could fight with his friends, as it is part of human relationships. Still, he never said hurtful things to them again. The three always had paper and a marker to write messages of encouragement to whoever needed it.

Words have power; you can use them for good or evil, and if you give messages of encouragement, you can change someone else's day.

Be careful what you say and try not to hurt others with your words; there are things you can say that will hurt others, and you decide if you say them to fill them with joy.

A Wild Ride And a Painful Lesson

Disobedience has painful consequences. Do you like pets? How well do you do with obedience? This story teaches you the consequences of not obeying a simple order.

Isaac loved visiting his grandparents whenever he had some days off from school. Their house was a bit far from his, on the city's outskirts. When he went, he enjoyed helping his grandfather pick the huge

zucchini, green beans, cucumbers, and giant pumpkins that grew there. In the summer, buckets were filled with fruit from the garden, but of all the things he loved, the most was feeding Rosy, the mare they had at home, who was beautiful.

She was a beautiful animal with very black, large eyes that looked like giant marbles. They stared fixedly at you with eyelashes that could be the envy of any model. She began to move anxiously and happily from her shed when she saw Isaac. Her ears moved and seemed to want attention, and her muzzle made happy sounds because she wanted to be pampered, but she wanted most to be fed.

Although Isaac loved giving her food, his grandfather always told him,

"For you, Rosy, there is no more food today. You cannot eat more; it is enough."

Isaac found this curious, and one day his grandfather said to him,

"She will kick me out of this house if I let her. She just wants to eat and eat, this greedy mare."

Isaac always gave Rosy her favorite food whenever he could.

"Could you please give her a little more, just a tiny bit, and nothing more?" he begged, but his grandfather's answer was firm.

"No, you can't."

His grandfather always warned him not to overfeed the mare. He often brought the carrots that she liked; he had just acquired them fresh, and she loved them. She was never tired of them.

One day, after Isaac heard the grandfather's truck heading into the city, he took the bag of carrots that Rosy liked and went to the stable to give them to her. He brought them and stood next to the door.

But the grandfather had firmly closed the door before leaving, and the latch was too high for Isaac to reach and open it.

So, for a few minutes, he contemplated what to do and decided that he could climb those rough, splintered pieces of wood and, using the garden rakes, he could open that door in front of him. He climbed up and saw the mare anxiously moving her front legs from side to side.

Isaac was so absorbed in admiring the mare's beauty that he lost his balance and fell into the corral on top of the mare's back, grabbing onto her ears. The mare

was frightened by this and lifted her hooves, striking the gate open as if it were made of paper. A moment later, the hooves were fading away as Rosy trotted away.

With terror, Isaac clung to the mare. His little arms could not wrap around her neck, so he squeezed her ears and tightly pressed his legs together to avoid falling. The path was difficult, filled with a series of stones. Rosy neighed loudly as she trampled everything in her way. She trotted over some newly planted fields and carried a blanket around her head, which seemed to agitate her more and make her run faster. All the clothes were left on the ground, dirty, and trampled. It was a wild ride.

Then, without warning, the mare suddenly stopped, causing Isaac to fly over her and fall uncontrollably. As he landed in the middle of a plot filled with small cacti, he screamed in pain, which could be heard from all around. Rosy just saw him and, without making a sound, turned around and ran in another direction towards the hill and was soon out of sight.

When the grandmother heard Isaac scream like that, she ran out of the house to see what had happened. She was shocked to see such a scene—a complete disaster. She quickly realized what had happened

and knew that the boy was the protagonist of this chaos.

"Your grandfather won't be happy when he finds out about this and discovers that the mare has escaped," she said.

Isaac had no response, but he didn't have the head to think about that. He had more important things to worry about, like getting all the thorns out of his body. So, after the grandmother removed the last thorn, she sent him to bed to rest and prepare for the scolding from his grandfather.

Isaac couldn't bear the thought of seeing his grandfather's disappointed face. When he came home and saw everything, he looked devastated because his beloved Rosy had escaped.

That day, as the night fell, the wind seemed to blow through the trees. The radio station announced that a big storm was coming and that it was best for everyone to stay home. The wind howled through the windows, and the leaves scattered and spread fear among everyone. The grandfather left without saying anything.

Hours later, as heavy drops began to fall, the grandfather arrived in his truck with Rosy tied up in the back.

"I see that while I was out running an errand, a lot of things happened in this house," said the grandfather. "All the ranches in the area have garbage everywhere, and people are going crazy looking for their animals that ran away due to the thunder. Luckily, I found the mare just around the corner, eating peacefully."

The grandfather thought for a moment that everything that had happened was due to the chaos of the storm and the strong winds, but the grandmother knew that wasn't the case. Isaac was petrified, waiting for her to rat him out. Still, the grandmother thought the thorns in his butt were punishment enough for his mischief. So, she never told the grandfather anything about his wild ride on the mare or what happened around him.

For several weeks, Isaac couldn't sit properly without the help of something soft. He thought about that mischief for years; it had been costly, and he never disobeyed his grandfather again.

When adults forbid you from doing something, it's because they know the potential consequences that could happen. Not following their rules can leave you with thorns in your buttocks.

Made in the USA
Las Vegas, NV
22 October 2024

10256264R00056